PASSENGER

A Love Story

Pramila Le Hunte

Copyright © 2019 Pramila Le Hunte.

Author Photo by David Stroud, other images by Alla Sinha

All rights reserved. No part of this book may be reproduced, stored, or transmitted by any means—whether auditory, graphic, mechanical, or electronic—without written permission of the author, except in the case of brief excerpts used in critical articles and reviews. Unauthorized reproduction of any part of this work is illegal and is punishable by law.

This is a work of fiction. All of the characters, names, incidents, organizations, and dialogue in this novel are either the products of the author's imagination or are used fictitiously.

ISBN: 978-1-4834-9870-6 (sc)
ISBN: 978-1-4834-8883-7 (e)

Library of Congress Control Number: 2019902568

Because of the dynamic nature of the Internet, any web addresses or links contained in this book may have changed since publication and may no longer be valid. The views expressed in this work are solely those of the author and do not necessarily reflect the views of the publisher, and the publisher hereby disclaims any responsibility for them.

Any people depicted in stock imagery provided by Getty Images are models, and such images are being used for illustrative purposes only. Certain stock imagery © Getty Images.

Lulu Publishing Services rev. date: 05/17/2019

Preface
About the Playwright

Meet Prami, a slim, sari-clad first-year student ripened to a glow in the Indian sun. There's an *élan vital*, a perky, quirky quality, about her. Not many girls sweep around Cambridge on a green Raleigh bike, gown and silk sari flying like a pennant in the wind. Off her bike, behold her! Her rounded hips suggest curves that would make any belly dancer proud. Cut a dash, young girl; allow your navel to keep peeping. Go for adventure and daring.

I was born in 1938 in a Frontier family. In Kipling country, the 'Wild West' of India but even the British never took control.

Once the snows melt in the Khyber Pass, wild tribes from Afghanistan descend and spread fear. An uncle of mine was shot from a rooftop with a rifle in his hand. No place to raise a child.

With gumboot determinism, my father started an upwards trek in life, mining high-quality iron ore at the other end of India. I reckon my genes carry that ore, or perhaps the gumboots!

I will never allow myself to be the product of an arranged marriage. In India, parents undertake a major in searching for an appropriate son-in-law. As a scriptwriter, it amuses me to create a similar scenario in my mind. Imagine my grandfather questioning a young man:

Question: What job are you in?
Answer: Mining.
Question: What are you mining, gold?
Answer: I'm afraid not. Only iron ore.
Question: How can you dress my daughter in iron ore?
Answer: There is very little gold mined in India, but there are heaps of iron ore.
Question: How awfully metallic!
Answer: So is iron ore.

Touché, Daddy!

It was iron ore that won the battle. My parents were married soon after that interview. My aunts insist my grandparents had obtained my mother's consent. When they asked her whether she would consent to the marriage, Mother had grunted: "Humph!" Perhaps it was unseemly to come out with a yes lest it imply, *Yes, I quite fancy the man!*

My mother was established for life with that magic little grunt, "Humph!" Little cry, but so much wool? Not so little, for the cuddly bundle was me, born in the see-saw of history with Gandhi on one side and Hitler on the other.

Little Freedom Fighter during the Raj

This chit of a seven-year-old girl, knee-high to a grasshopper, starts her thespian life as a ready-made package with just a mighty two-word script, *Quit India*, acted by a gutsy, no-holds-barred performer.

The cast is British and Indian. We are in the last hurrah of the Raj, with Britain and India in conflict. What else can you expect in 1945, with Mountbatten's arrival around the corner and the sweet smell of impending freedom?

It's 1946, a year before independence. Gandhiji's final assault is in progress. He has instructed Indians to be resolute. Whenever they encounter a Britisher, they are to demand, "Quit India!" Now, an English friend and I play every afternoon in the tennis courts while both the ayah folk gossip.

I follow Gandhiji's injunction. "Quit India!" I shout, hurling a pebble from the tennis court. As to be expected, I get another stone back; my forehead bleeds! The British and Indians are officially now at war.

My parents are the only Indian residents in a white world. The denizens of this august place have been warned by their British bosses in Calcutta: "Mixing with Indians can only lead to trouble. Do you want Gandhi and his mob at your doorstep, old chap?"

But the boss of my tennis courts doesn't mind. Yes, he would like to open the door to the little dhoti, and his wife confirms she'll give him a cup of the very best Welsh tea. Tea is a product of India, so I too want to give the dhoti the very best tea. My parents talk of little else but Mahatma Gandhi.

As might be expected, the incident magnifies with each telling. As is natural with the metamorphosis of rumour, my antics become epic: the valour of a lone Indian girl and the defeat of the mighty!

A congress worker persuades the locals to convert the Wednesday afternoon cockfight at the market into a confrontation between a white leghorn cockerel and a colourful multiplumed specimen from the jungle. A large group of men, eyes red and swollen with toddy, form a ring, while women, with sweet frangipani in their hair, sway to the hypnotic *thump, thump* of the tribal drums.

The Colosseum of the Indies is preparing for a festival, a fight unto the death.

And that's the way history unfolds. It is also the past of the principal character in the play *Gore Baba*. He too is a latter-day Gandhi, but he casts no stones. "Kill no birds" is his mantra of nonviolence, and I, a committed Gandhian, threw the first stone!

Our home is Gandhian. I am wearing dresses made of khadi, a material entirely hand spun and handwoven.

Gandhiji had said that the British stole our cotton crops and sent them off to Britain to be spun into beautiful fabric that English women wear in the clubs of Calcutta. In a similar British playground, Auntyji, my scheming doyen of Calcutta, holds court. I portray her as an infamous relic of the Raj. The new India that emerges is a funny old place: jingle bells and temple bells call out together; high-society club life and roguish street life throb, with monkey dancers and pickpockets on the make. Not just Great Britain but India, too, has a case to answer. It was an Indian who assassinated our great leader.

The most defining day in my life was certainly the assassination of Mahatma Gandhi on 30 January 1948. Although I was just nine years old at the time, the news made me grow up in a day. I had seen Gandhiji and had even gone to a prayer meeting when he was in Calcutta. I remember him as a bent old man who somehow managed to walk very fast.

A stunned nation listened to the voice of Melville de Mellow as he gave a seven-hour live commentary of Gandhi's death.

> I shuddered when I saw the bullet-wounds—dark ominous patches of hate and madness. ... As I gazed at that face, words raced through my mind slowly penetrating the numbness of body. Soul-words I had learnt so well in my childhood. Words that Jesus Christ used on the Cross: "Father forgive them; for they know not what they do." Bapu's lips seemed to be moving and saying just that. ... As I stood there in silence, someone near me tried unsuccessfully to hold back a

sob. I turned my head to look straight into the tortured face of India's Prime Minister, Pandit Jawaharlal Nehru. I left quietly, left behind for a moment the greatest man of our age in that room of tears, tragedy and rose-petals.[1]

I, the little girl, grew up as expected and climbed upwards like my father on a green Raleigh bike that I named the Green Monster.

Let's see where it goes.

The Greenhorn Teacher, the Big Teacher

But first things first: I must find a school for my father's staff. I work for him now in his jungle. I am now a graduate of Cambridge, a trained teacher from Simla, with the same daring that showed at the tennis courts of yore.

My father has risen high in his mining business and is considered a pillar of the community. I now need a school for his staff, but there is no English school here, and he's losing his best people.

I imagine a space, a line of whitewashed staff quarters, a little veranda in front, a courtyard at the back leading on to an outside loo. Now, add an ayah, a carpenter, and a plumber, and you have a school. As easy as that! But what about a teacher? Who on earth would migrate to the sticks?

I fish in a national paper and locate one. She takes up post as headmistress, bringing along a husband and five children! For me, where there's a will, there's a way. For her, where there's a need, a way will be found. Both husband and wife are out of work. She can do the teaching stuff, and I'll lend a hand with dramatics. The end-of-year show is *Cinderella*, which I direct. To tell the truth, the school itself is a Cinderella story.

---

[1] Melville de Mellow, "Reminiscences of Gandhi: The Last Journey" (10 Feb. 1948), http://www.gandhi-manibhavan.org/eduresources/chap3.htm, accessed 31 January 2019.

The show ends with a roaring chorus worthy of Broadway:

> Found a peanut, found a peanut,
> Found a peanut just now.
> It was rotten, it was rotten, it was rotten just now.
> Got a tummy ache, got a tummy ache, got a tummy ache just now.
> Had an operation, had an operation, had an operation just now.
> Doctor said I'd live, doctor said I'd live,
> doctor said I'd live just now!

(To be sung to the tune of "Clementine")

No one got a tummy ache. Of course you'll live, my little school. This trusty peanut will take you forward with a munch-crunch determinism.

Of all my life's later successes, I regard opening this school to be my most significant achievement.

At the end of the year, each class was promoted in the hope that over the years the school would burst at the seams. It has done more than that. It is now a flourishing institution that sends buses to collect students from the neighbouring districts, and what is more important, it makes sure that the tribal children receive a quality education. Didn't the doctor say, "You'll live, little peanut"?

A Green Monster Bicycle Ride

Put me back on the bicycle, and let me take you for the ride of a lifetime.

> Spurr'd boldly on and dash'd through thick and thin,
> Through sense and nonsense, never out nor in;
> Free from all meaning whether good or bad,
> And in one word, heroically mad.[2]

---
[2] From John Dryden's *Absalom and Achtiophel*.

I'm a graduate now, married to a Welshman. It is now my turn to educate my four children.

The leaves are turning colour, and the wheat is harvested—haystacks of gold! Keats calls this a season of mists and mellow fruitfulness; it augurs well.

It's September 1968. Like a rush, the storm breaks furious when I drop my children off at school in a sari. It is an inglorious autumn for them because, despite the school being in an elitist area, Asian children receive the sting of caustic racial abuse. The country then was not the multicultural Britain of today. Colour prejudice was digging deep, warning the English of arriving immigrants.

"Like the Roman, I seem to see the river Tiber foaming with much blood." This line comes from the *Aeneid*. A political speech Enoch Powell delivered in Birmingham to the Conservative Political Centre on 20 April 1968 was later given the title "Rivers of Blood", alluding to this line.

Within the space of only five months, the tinder has been lit. Yes, the Far Right is about. "Paki!" the children spit out, but to me those to whom they're referring look Caucasian. I tell the children that clothes don't matter; it's people who count. But what people! This *riff-raff* word comes to the children's lips easily enough. It must be what they now hear all around.

Busy with picking holes in English children, it is now I who must face the ugly truth. I don't want my daughter playing with a neighbour who is a plumber's daughter. In India, sweepering is a low-caste profession.

I look in the mirror darkly. I have come to settle in England. Have I carried my filthy prejudice as baggage?

It befits me to fit into the system. Time for a miniskirt—allow my airy thighs to freeze.

Fortunately, I have a curriculum vitae to warm me. I am already a qualified teacher, now rubber-stamped "MA (Cantab)". The highway is open. I find myself as the head of English at the most prestigious school in the country. We don't do peanuts here but plum pudding, served best at Oxbridge.

It's been two years since my dearest father passed away, and my mother is finding it difficult to face his loss. She has made his bedside table a shrine. The comb in the drawer is exactly where he left it, and his medication is neatly placed in the drawer. She wants to grieve by stopping the clock. But I have to grieve my way. I've been an active little politician from the start. I fling myself into local politics with Prami-style determinism. Except you just don't wear gumboots with miniskirts. You have to wear trendy boots.

Richmond is controlled by the Liberals. I observe boring council meetings and enter Richmond's mindset. However, to get noticed, I need a cause. There is a great deal of scope. Everybody keeps cutting costs these days. Even the old bench in my park will be removed. I write a ballad in its defence that I distribute as flyers. My first script, as I like to call it, is loaded with the jetsam of politics.

> I have a repertoire noire
> Of corruption in power.
> Old timbers remember a lot.
> When motorbike recruits in their steel-tipped boots
> Volley and thunder my ground,
> The pub shuts its doors. A vagrant snores
> Beneath sheets of newspaper dies he.
> Poor Tom. I knew him well.
> He was a war hero.
> He defended a bridge near Two Sister's Ridge

When the Falkland battle was won.
Not a verse nor a prayer was read by the mayor.
But a photo op soon came along!
I'll expose the guile
Behind his smile.

Heed every word that he said:
"Morals aside, we've nothing to hide.
Our actions are pure as this snow.
We've said with one voice
We don't have a choice.
This scheming old bench must go!
She'll rally her supporters
Along with reporters
And demand that our council must go!

With elections around us, we can't let her hound us.
We'll take action with stealth, bring in issues of health,
And order the reporters to go!
We'll start a big fire then sneek away from the pyre
And put it down to the blacks next door!
And later, the whole park can go!"

As the adrenalin flows, my ambition rises. If a battleground is required, then let it not come from a bench in the park. It's Parliament that must hear me; therefore, "Cry 'Havoc!', and let slip the dogs of war."[3]

I won the SWAN award for the most original production of the year, for *Tamburlaine*, Christopher Marlowe's tale of the mighty conqueror. I have always been a theatre person.

To my joy I get to direct my beloved Shakespeare's *Much Ado about Nothing*. No, it's not about nothing; it's a great to-do about myself.

---

[3] From William Shakespeare's *Julius Caesar*.

As You Like It? Of course they'll like it. I'm a bloody great director. Besides, it's set in a forest where supposedly the deer weeps by the brook. But from experience, I very well know what really goes on in the woods. Art, holds a mirror to Nature; *Measure for Measure*? Well, one should get what one deserves, and surprisingly it happens.

Hearing of my success, the Arts Council of Richmond approaches me to direct a world premiere of Shakespeare's *The Tempest*.

"A world premiere!" I gasp. "It's unbelievable. The world has done all of Shakespeare before!"

But not, it turned out, with Sir Arthur Sullivan's additions. He used the might of a full orchestra for just a few minutes of the opening storm, composed for operatic voices and four-part harmony, leaving out all titbits of conspiracy that actually tell the story. In the end, the play becomes a commercial white elephant. Would I take this challenge on?

"Of course!" I turn into a new-born evangelist for the arts. Creation is all! I shall get the Royal Ballet School to dance the rest.

"Can she have it all?" writes Valerie Grove in *The Compleat Woman*, a collection of twelve biographies of successful women who have gotten "there" with at least four children underfoot. Have I gotten there, really? Once, getting there meant admission to Cambridge. Now, I can have my cake and eat it.

Am I getting too arrogant? Will pride have a fall?

No, the Queen Bee coronation happens yet again. To my astonishment. I have been asked to join a committee set up by the Secretary of State to design a more comprehensive profile of the English language itself. Of all the English teachers in the country, only two were selected as flag-bearers of our subject, and it was yours truly who was given the voice, a girl once punished by her mother for "weak academic performance", in other words, not knowing the difference between transitive and intransitive verbs. There has to be black irony somewhere in this, eh? It was our committee that brought grammar back into the curriculum.

I'm getting ready for rehearsal for my bionic *Tempest* to wow them all. But Fate steps in. Yes, pride will have a fall. Margaret Thatcher has called a general election, and I happen to be a candidate for a city in West Midland. I put my tail between my legs. "Yes, my country is all."

Glimpses from the Hustings General Election, Thursday, 9 June 9 1983

My constituency is feverish, powered by the chutzpah of the moment, because I'm the first Indian woman appearing as a Conservative candidate. Media follow me around as an oddity, a candidate for the stocks—all because I support Margaret Thatcher, not the flavour of the day.

"If you turn up near a polling booth, you're a dead duck!"

The run-up to the polling day gets worse. I am standing on an open van in Indian dress, trying to address the crowds gathered around, mainly Asians, when suddenly a stone is thrown violently at me, grazing my temple. I feel surrounded by a fairground of hate. Although terrified, I know I cannot back down.

My constituency lies in the heart of the city. All around, one can see the impact of prestigious businesses. Extraordinary that such posh surroundings are inhabited by ladies of the night!

On my way back to my lodging, I pull in by a curb to meet these women and take in their complaints. The police move them on, but all the women can do is to shift to another road, where the same trouble starts again. I can do nothing for those of the world's oldest profession, but I have to become a buddy, *simpatico*. No politician has done that before. As a teacher, I get them to open up about their children and the problems of raising a family given their working hours. I suggest the meerkat model: one stands watch while others forage. They enjoy a buddy laugh.

Mine is a heavily multiethnic community, and that might well be the reason for my choice. The heartland contains several Sikh temples whose adherents have awakened to the huge publicity surrounding me. I happen to be the first Indian woman chosen by the Conservative Party. A leader orders his menfolk to be alongside at all times, but I cannot be associated with just one group. I take a chance and spread myself around. My constituency is replete with high-rise, run-down flats filled with the unemployed. Needless to say, knocking on doors for Thatcher is traumatic. The woman is not the flavour of the day. One man sets his dog on me!

Back in India, Prime Minister Indira Gandhi is facing trouble with the Sikhs in Punjab, who are demanding their own separate state. Although resident in England, my Sikhs have left their hearts in Punjab. They want to give voice to their giant diaspora and persuade Indira to steer off Sikh affairs. Coach after coach sets off for Hyde Park, where they plan a gathering of more than thirty-five thousand Sikhs. The leader invites me to the rostrum. I'm caught between a rock and a hard place. I'm here to see to Thatcher's needs, not to appear on vagrant diversions. Yet these are the very folk who will comprise my grass-roots support. How can grass be greener somewhere else in Delhi? I have never spoken to such a large gathering, and my Punjabi is pathetic! But come the time, the performer in me emerges. What an experience! Loudspeaker behind loudspeaker relays my voice.

Finally, I gain access to Azad Kashmir households of Mirpur in the Himalayas, where no candidate had previously entered. I, knowing

Urdu, can do a little job for their pubescent daughters, who must be returned home because the school uniform, or even trousers, is not acceptable, being most revealing of shape. Elementary, my dear Maggie. I now have connections. The council need not require girls to tuck uniform blouses into trousers; just allow them to hang out. Invisible bottoms!

Then, I exchange my Punjabi suits for Western clothing. For the leafy suburbs, a twinset and pearls are a must. A shared tipple of sherry seals the deal. I might even offer one to *Auntyji* of my play while she plans her party at the club.

So, life goes on; the wheel turns around. I go to India and back, where I write for an Indian audience, Bollywood in mind!

For one knocked already by two stones, I expect a third will follow; everything comes in threes. This one comes from a different direction.

My husband is filing for divorce. The marriage didn't work out. You win some, you lose some; that's life.

> I am good, but not an angel. I do sin, but I am not the devil. I am just a small girl in a big world trying to find someone to love.
> —Marilyn Monroe

The Next Step on the Wooden O

> The lyf so short, the craft so longe to lerne.
> Th' assay so hard, so sharp the conquerynge,
> The dredful joye, alwey that slit so yerne;
> Al this mene I be love.[4]

As Chaucer says, life is so short and the craft so long to learn, yet so rewarding because it is a labour of love.

---

[4] From Geoffrey Chaucer's *Parlement of Foules*.

Past eighty now, this woman is still young enough to pick up the pen again. My Green Monster has taken my plays all over, but now it's a pussycat by the hearth. I titled my play *Passenger*, because aren't we all passengers of life? Allow me take a last bow and pull the curtain down.

Passenger is an endearing romance. An English girl and an English boy find each other, and themselves, cocooned in a historical space in Calcutta, where I grew up. They are guided into their future by a mysterious stranger, a little rouge, a sugar and salt philosopher, a latter-day Gandhi.

I have a dream. I hope *Passenger* will inspire you to consider the large issues that plague our society, like racism, prejudice, the sorry left outs of society in our midst, misguided nationalism leading to war, and the role education might play to combat this plague. I have made a video available for people to use.

> Life is a great big canvas. Throw all the paint you can.
> —Danny Kaye

As Mother Teresa says, we can't change the world, but we can try. It is my plea to the young people of today to plant their footsteps firmly in the shifting sands of tomorrow. My Raleigh bicycle might have punctured, but the traffic won't stop. Don't be compromised by the forbidding double yellow lines. It's the system, my friend. Keep pedalling.

I thank my father. A pioneer in sola topi, he tramped the jungles unafraid.

The green berries of the mahua tree have ripened. Their pungent odour permeates deep within the jungle and, like the tiger's mating scent, invites the lugubrious sloth bears, snugged in their caves, to startle and attend. The approaching dawn awaits their festival! Generously scattered green mahua berries ferment with the rising heat. Surfeiting on a feast of liquor, the bears start to dance!

Acknowledgements

My thanks to
Dilip Shankar, for being my right-hand man all the time.
Theresa Maher, for being my right-hand woman all the time.
Anita Barnes, for reading the script.
Bem Le Hunte, for giving me feedback on the script.
Paradise Green, for a super venue to perform
Alia Sinha, for her original illustrations
Mary Wallace Theatre and Pinner Village Hall
Uma Prakash, for publicity
David Stroud, for the photograph
Mrinalini Chawla, for the poster
Consulate of India

Poster for *Passenger*

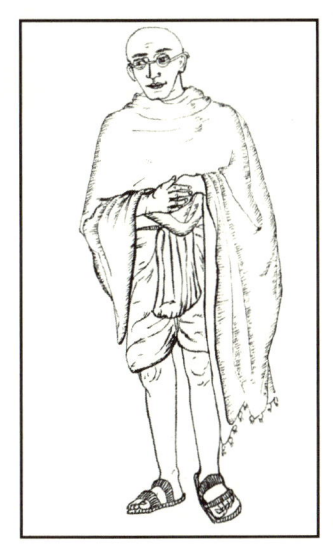

A historical play set in the middle of the twentieth century when the British rulers of India were thrown out by Gandhi and when Indians of all classes surged in to fill the vacuum created by the British departure. It was also a time when a vigorous Anglo-Indian community flourished in Calcutta. Now, this great culture is almost a memory.

A play of love for those who care for the wonder of the world we live in and all the people who share this great planet. This story is designed to inspire the young people of today to move forward with hope and step forward to play their parts in the world of tomorrow.

Dedicated to my husband Bill Le Hunte, who joined me during these historic changeover times but passed away even as I penned these lines.

Synopsis

I wish to reach out to schools and colleges and all those who care to invest in our beautiful young people. With this in mind I have chosen two young people, Wendy and Charles, to be my young ambassadors of goodwill.

Passenger is an endearing romance that reaches the heart of everyone, young or old. An English girl and boy, Wendy and Charles, find each other, and themselves, cocooned in a historical space in Calcutta when Britain moves out and the new constitution of India is not yet born. They arrive in Calcutta for different reasons. During her childhood at the time of the British Raj, Wendy lived in India and suffered the trauma of savage religious violence when India was divided, as the British left India, into two countries, India and Pakistan. But she has forgotten it all. In fact, she has lost in touch with her own identity. Therefore, she seeks herself, and is helped by Baba, masquerading ironically as a fake religious upstart, a latter-day Gandhi of the streets. He jumps into the story as mentor of the young Wendy who will guide her on a journey of self-discovery, unpeeling like an onion the problems of being an Anglo-Indian in the high society of British India, where being of mixed breed is fodder for all.

Wendy will be tested mentally and emotionally by attempted rape coming from a British polo player. But in reality, Baba is a highly learned philosopher who has converted from being a radical freedom fighter to becoming the flag-bearer of cherished Indian values of the great philosopher Swami Vivekananda, who has tried to create a bridge between the East and the West with his message that all religions are true.

Charles has come across the writings of this great guru and has come to immerse himself in the sanctuary of Vivekananda's ministry at Belur Math and take his message back to a Europe dismembered by the war.

Wendy and Charles are guided into their future by a mysterious stranger who brings humour and high drama into their lives.

I feel that Baba, wily and saintly at the same time, is the litmus that will expose the blackness of newly arrived freedom, the quagmire of the emerging new India with its discrimination against transgender people and victims of disease like the outcast lepers side by side by the exclusive elite who inhabit the Victoria Club, synonymous with the British "at play" in clubs in India. Therefore, please also meet the evil base of high society, the mother and son team of Auntyji and Rohan, who will connive to keep alive the fantasy of the British Raj and by their lust for power and position—even if it could lead to murder!

A picaresque duo, they will add the zing, the masala as we call it, to the black humour of the story.

However, the bottom line enunciates the importance of love for humankind and country as enunciated by Swami Vivekananda that compellingly warns against the terror of war.

Discussions and debates can and *must* be generated after introduction of the play, either by reading or production, to examine the larger issues that plague our society, like racism, class division, and misguided nationalism, and the role education might play to prepare young people to combat this plague.

Nevertheless, it is a play for enjoyment per se, even though I might have smuggled serious issues that teachers and educationists might like to use.

I am a playwright, teacher, and theatre director who grew up in Calcutta during the time in which the play is set. I gloried in the opportunity the new India offered but cried at the bloodshed that paved its way. *Passenger* is a plea to the young people of today to plant their footsteps firmly in the shifting sands of tomorrow. I have a video of both the play and selected scenes connected with the theme that can be purchased along with the book.

Characters

Baba A fair-skinned, highly educated middle-aged man with spiritual leanings. Wily and spiritual, this scholar is the pulse of new India, mixing alike with high society powerhouse Moguls and afflicted lepers in colonies. He will go to any means to achieve his honourable ends.

Wendy A confused English girl who returns to India to find her identity. She goes on a journey of self-discovery with Baba. She comes to terms with her Anglo-Indian origins. Her story exposes the racism inherent in both pre-Raj and post-Raj India.

Charles Friend of Wendy; now gone radical. Very troubled about the postwar Western world. He too take a journey of self-development, but he does so in a monastery and serves as his own guide. He could carry a guitar or a violin.

Eventually, the two young people are inspired by Baba to march to the beat of the same drum.

Auntyji The club, a hangover from the British Raj, is hub of upper-class India, and Auntyji, the chairperson of the club, is a matriarch of some stature. Her ambition can be overreaching, especially given that her origins are humble. She would like her son to marry a posh British girl.

Rohan Auntyji's layabout son. He is a junior version of his mother as far as snobbery is concerned. But there is a darker side to him.

Mrs Bannerji A member of the Victoria Club. Ready to stab in the back at the first opportunity.

Hijra A transgender person who was born male. Now officially recognised as "third gender", transgender people like Hijra dance and beg for survival. Traditionally hijras were invited to bless new-born babies and weddings.

Amita Bose Budding reporter; wants to find a "true" story for her paper.

Gypsy Woman A soothsayer who has dark visions of the future.

Mohammed A street rogue.

Mali Gardener of Auntyji.

Historical Information

Swami Vivekananda (1863–1902) Indian philosopher and thinker, disciple of Ramakrishna Paramhansa, pioneer of interfaith awareness and equality.

Belur Math Headquarters of Ramakrishna Mission, Calcutta.

Ganges (or Holy Ganga) Major river; flows into Bay of Bengal; called Hooghly in Calcutta.

Ayah Nurse, child-care provider; almost a godmother.

Anglo-Indians During the centuries when Britain was in India, the children born to British men and Indian women began to form a new community. They made up a small but significant portion of the population during the British Raj and were well represented in certain administrative roles.

New Market Vibrant market in the heart of Calcutta and vital to its cultural fabric.

Sadhu Mendicant who has renounced the world.

Independence Day 15 August 1947.

We condemn the starless night of racism and intend no offence to any community, nationality, race, species, religion, belief, or individual.

SCENE 1
Newmarket

Sound of fireworks. Singing of "Jai he, jai he, jaya, jaya, jaya he" (the Indian national anthem)

Enter AMITA, MOHAMMED, *and* HIJRA

AMITA

Independence Day! The war is over! Queen Elizabeth's coronation is over. There are fireworks flying and celebrations in New Market, and there are British tourists all around. I must find a story for my newspaper, or else my editor will sack me! I'm only a trainee journalist. How the hell do I find a story?

MOHAMMED *and* HIJRA *dance.* AMITA *walks into their light expectantly*

To MOHAMMED

Salaam alaikum!

MOHAMMED

Walaikum salaam!

AMITA

You look happy!

MOHAMMED

Very happy. White skin is like an ointment that can easily be rubbed off.

HIJRA and MOHAMMED freeze

AMITA

Moves away from the dancers

That will make a sensational story: Mohammedan kills Hijra on Independence Day! I can see myself on camera: Amita Bose, Fake News. But how can he kill the Hijra if he is dancing? I'll be found out! I must look out for a true story somewhere else.

Enter BABA, dressed in a short dhoti

Ah! There's Gandhi on the streets of Calcutta five years after his death. Whom is he trying to deceive? I'll expose him.

Crosses over towards BABA

BABA

> [Reads] "Wendy reaching Independence Day. STOP. Abandoned university. STOP. Forgotten her Calcutta life [I'm not surprised]. STOP. Take good care of her. [Of course]. STOP. Trust you completely. [Trust me? *Me?* That's taking a risk ...] STOP. Belinda Jones." Her mother—my friend.
>
> The last time I saw Wendy, she was a little girl tucked into the folds of her ayah's sari—so sweet, so perfect. *Love immense and infinite, broad as the sky and deep as the ocean.* And now her mother has sent her to me! Something must have happened in the past when she lived in the compound of the British Embassy. I must help this child, try to get into her past. No more British, but there's still the club ...

AMITA

> [Aside] This Gandhi will do the job. A story lurking!
>
> *Steps forward*
>
> Excuse me. Why are you dressed like Gandhi?

BABA

> *Brushes her off, irritated*
>
> Later!
>
> *A bus horn sounds*
>
> That must be Wendy!
>
> *Exit*

AMITA

I'm not going to let this Gandhi get away!

Enter WENDY, *who bumps into* AMITA, *who immediately takes out her notebook. Hello welcome. Tell me all about you. Why are you here on this wonderful day?*

In the beginning, WENDY *feels important for being questioned by a journalist, but then she gets restless and starts looking for* CHARLES

HIJRA and MOHAMMED

Dancing with abandon around WENDY *and* AMITA, *singing*

Tourist, tourist. Money, money.

WENDY *acts restless, releases herself from* AMITA

AMITA

One thing I know for sure is that this Wendy is not British. There has to be a story behind her.

WENDY walks around looking for CHARLES

WENDY

Charles! Charles! Where are you?

HIJRA and MOHAMMED parrot WENDY

Enter CHARLES. HIJRA and MOHAMMED pull CHARLES aside to dance. A tug of war ensues between WENDY and the dancers, with CHARLES in the middle

WENDY

Charles, Charles!

During the dance, HIJRA tries to pick CHARLES's pocket. WENDY pulls CHARLES to the side and shoos HIJRA and MOHAMMED away

WENDY

Bhago. Bhago. Go away!

To CHARLES

You blithering idiot! You don't know it here—it's not like bloody Cambridge! You have to stay away from the riff-raff!

AMITA

There's something going on between them, that's for sure!

Laughs

If I get more material, I'll probably write a novel. Amita, keep looking!

CHARLES

> Wendy! Have you seen the streets lined up with all sorts of things, snake charmers, women of the trade…

WENDY

> Is that what you are interested in?!

CHARLES

> Um…

WENDY

> Let me show you the New Market I knew when I lived here.

> and where my ayah used to take me, secretly, to give sweets to little beggars.

> *Exeunt.* AMITA *follows, looking curious*

AMITA

> *Opens her notebook*

> [To herself, with excitement] Secretly to beggars!

Sees BABA *and turns around*

But first things first!

Enter BABA, *searching for* WENDY. AMITA *readies herself and then approaches* BABA *with confidence*

Why are you so fake?

BABA

After all this is New Market—the hunting ground for fakes.

Sits cross-legged

Fakeness is a virtue—digest it if you can—seldom found in a woman and always in a man. Look, I am posing as the expected astrologer, sitting cross-legged beside a mat of half-understood charts and symbols, one eye closed for meditation, the other open for business.

Mimes comically

Now leave me alone. I have to find my Wendy.

AMITA

[With triumph] Wendy Fotherington Jones!

BABA

How do you know her?

AMITA

We journalists have our ways!

Exit, teasingly chuffed

Enter WENDY *and* CHARLES. BABA *overhears their conversation*

WENDY

[With disappointment] I don't like New Market. India has changed since I lived here!

BABA

Rises forward

Don't weep for India. Don't get upset about shouting matches and baby snatches—they happen all over the world. The British had a go at this country, but the body fought back. The heart still beats with the rugged rhythm of life that you don't recognise.

CHARLES

    [Aggressively] Who are you?!

BABA

    I am Baba. And you must be … (dismissively) whatever you are? But she is Wendy.

    Hands WENDY *the telegram*

WENDY

    [Reads] You must be Babaji! My mother told me all about you.

    Touches BABA's *feet awkwardly*

CHARLES

    [Aside, snidely] She stoops to conquer!

WENDY

    [With irritation] Shut up! Have manners!

    CHARLES *smirks*

BABA

    The telegram didn't say anything about a young man.

    Looks CHARLES *straight in the eye then turns his face to* WENDY

    How well I remember you, sweet one! A tender babe in my arms.

    CHARLES *snatches the telegram angrily.* BABA *looks at him suspiciously*

WENDY

What an alarmist my mother is! She told me you worked alongside her in Varanasi, with lepers. Maybe that's why she contacted you. You are very kind, sir, but there is no need to worry about me. I've lived in India before. I can find my way round. And this is Charles, my travelling companion.

CHARLES

The best of the morning to you, sir.

BABA

"Do not think it's morning and dismiss it with a name. See it for the first time as a new born child that has no name."

WENDY

[Taken in by the quotation, muses] Yes that's what I want to be, a child, new born. That's why I returned to India, to find myself. I don't feel like Wendy Fotherington Jones.

CHARLES

I thought you were Wendy Jones!

BABA

When a bird leaves its nest it tries to fly directly towards her mother but in your case, your mother felt that a home for lepers was too harsh for a growing child. You were given a new home with soft feathers—the Fotherington home. And now, with your foster parents dead, where would you go?

WENDY

>I …

CHARLES

>[Jokingly] Be careful. Have you heard of Miss Starkey?
>There once was a girl called Starkey
>Who had an affair with a darky.
>The result of their sins
>Was triplets, not twins—
>One white, one black, and one khaki.

WENDY

>Charles!

CHARLES

>That's what happens when soldiers get around!

WENDY

>How can you say such things!

CHARLES

>National Service at your service! The look in your eyes suggests that I have emerged from the gutter. I'm not an arsehole.

WENDY

>[Amused, forgetting her critical response to CHARLES] Oh! A monkey dancer and his two monkeys; let's go see them! I was never allowed to do so before.

>*Rushes off*

CHARLES

>And I shall play for them a jaunty tune on my violin. Did you know I teach the stuff?
>
>*Exit* WENDY, *motioning to* CHARLES

BABA

>*A little suspicious, forcefully stopping* CHARLES
>
>How well do you know Wendy?

CHARLES

>[Casually] Not too well. I answered an ad she'd put out at university. "And I being poor have only my dreams. So tread carefully, for you tread on my dreams." And I've brought my dreams to Calcutta. From talking to her on the plane, I got the idea she's a rags-to-riches girl.

BABA

>*Moves closer to* CHARLES *and holds his collar*
>
>You must have known she was connected with diplomats.
>
>CHARLES *nods*
>
>You're not after her money, by any chance?

CHARLES

>*Throws up his hands*
>
>God forbid! I was only speaking in metaphor when I said from rags to riches.

BABA

> There can be no metaphor for rags. They are real—torn bits of clothing lepers use as bandages to hide their deformities, their rotted-away fingers and toes. They always leak blood. And their tragic history is written on their faces.

CHARLES

> *Reacting with strong body language*
>
> Rotted limbs? We are so sanitised in Britain. I can't even begin to imagine …

BABA

> I have worked with lepers. It's a pity you can't even face the thought.

CHARLES

> I'm sorry, Baba, but this image, it doesn't go away. She might have been beautiful once. But look at her now. Maybe her fingers and toes …

BABA

Yes, they are most probably rotted.

CHARLES shudders

Reality slapping you in the face, hitting you in your comfort zone? Hmm?

Charles

[Impulsively] Will you take me to see these lepers? I can take horror on the chin.

BABA

[Whispers] This is idle curiosity, Charles. You don't just see them; you learn from them.

Exit

Enter WENDY, excited

WENDY

Charles, I've just seen the monkeys dancing around in the market! Come dance with me. I'll show you. They are so cute!

Enter HIJRA, dancing, approaching WENDY, whom he has been watching. HIJRA catches WENDY's arm and puts a necklace around her neck. Another vendor, MOHAMMED, has followed HIJRA and is watching, waiting for his opportunity

HIJRA

You look like the Queen!

WENDY

No thank you!

Takes the necklace off and tries to return it

HIJRA

No return! These are blessings from Himalayas. Now she'll have a hundred babies. All boys!

HIJRA wants money. Eventually CHARLES must give him some coins

CHARLES

Buy some sweets.

HIJRA

More money! Otherwise …

Starts to lift his sari

CHARLES gets out more money and hands it to HIJRA

HIJRA begins to leave

CHARLES

Begging, begging, begging!

HIJRA

Stops

What else someone like me can do?

Exit

MOHAMMED

If she wants *boys*, the best place is my new desert country, West Pakistan. No weak-limbed, fish-eating, dal-eating, dal-farting Hindu would be man enough to father so many sons.

Moves towards WENDY

British lady, come with me. I'm a great warlord from Baluchistan. My wives will take care of you. They will put oil on you and place a four-carat diamond pin in your nose.

CHARLES

Tosses MOHAMMED *a coin*

Go off and find your camel. I promise on the word of an English gentleman.

Tries to shoo off Mohammed

Exit CHARLES *and* WENDY

Enter BABA CLOSELY FOLLOWED BY AMITA.

MOHAMMED

Baba, is this journalist still chasing you?

BABA

Amita Bose, Amita Bose, why are you still chasing me? I told you I'll tell you everything later. This is not the time.

AMITA

> Oh, you never have time!

BABA

> How can I have time? I am an entrepreneur—work as a priest for a very rich woman of Calcutta.

MOHAMMED

> [Cheekily] Auntyji. We all know her and keep out of her way. She kicks with her high-heel shoes.

BABA

> Maybe, but she can be of use!
>
> *To MOHAMMED*
>
> Won't share any of it with you, rogue. No! Auntyji will be useful if I conduct the orchestra of what will follow.
>
> *Starts off like an orchestra conductor, raising his baton*
>
> *Music (Balero by Ravel)*
>
> Wendy's mother has asked me to help her—and my little girl needs to go to the club! Auntyji is chairperson of the club. And she has given me money to find an English rose to parade as the bride for her son! But Rohan, her son, has also done that; she for bride, he for bed.
>
> *Starts writing in capital letters on a small slip of paper he has pulled out from a knot in his dhoti and speaks as he writes suitable girl found. Wendy Fotherington I shall have to write*

in capital letters because she is a simple village girl not properly educated.

Hands it to MOHAMMED.

Mohammed! Take this to Auntyji at Victoria Club. Big memsahib there. Here, take your money!

Exit MOHAMMED

BABA *collapses*

Plan in action!

Enter CHARLES *and* WENDY, *with books*

WENDY

(Giggles)

Baba, what have you been up to? Look, we went to a book shop. I bought a Mills and Boon *Hot and Bothered*. Charles bought a boring history book.

BABA

Which book?

CHARLES

Train to Pakistan.

WENDY

That's fiction—one man's view on the Partition.

CHARLES

> The largest mass migration in history!

BABA

> The greatest number of murders.

CHARLES

> Over a million dead.

BABA

> [Sharply] Not just facts and numbers, *but the reason. The worst thing you can do with dogma is to give it an empire.* Become a journalist. Find the truth!

CHARLES

> "What is truth?" asked a jesting Pilate, not staying around long enough for an answer. I've tried that already. I've looked at people. *I've been to the ducks swimming in the pond, and they won't come to be killed, Mrs Bond!*

BABA

> Nobody likes to die. The reality is, they are killed. You must investigate the truth. Why don't you start with Wendy? She was there! Wendy, what do you remember of the Partition?

WENDY

> [Stutters] I don't remember anything. I was a little girl. I remember playing with Sarah.

BABA

> Not everything was play, Wendy! There was a war going on!

WENDY

> A war was going on. We had blackouts and siren practice that frightened me,

BABA

> A Japanese invasion?

WENDY

> There was some talk about a Japanese invasion. And large silver balloons floating in the sky. We carefully pulled our curtains closed at night. Sarah and I played hide-and-seek in the dark. It was such fun.

BABA

> Think! Why did you pull the curtains down?

CHARLES

> Bombs!

BABA

> You were with me during the Calcutta killings just a day before India became independent. Mr Fotherington had sent you to me for safe custody ...

CHARLES

> Wouldn't she have been better off in a white precinct?

BABA

> No. Even the servants knew that she was not British, that she was an Anglo-Indian intruder. Anyone could have reported her.

Holding on tightly to WENDY

> It was a horrifying day. As bricks were thrown nonstop at the temple where we were hiding, we began to see, through the smashed windows, red dust filling the air. It was choking us. *Very dramatic.* We feared that the next one to come might smash our heads. You crushed yourself against my shoulder.

But the wardens of the temple, the priests, fought back. The police say that thirty Mohammedans were killed in front of us. Amidst the shrieking and the clamour, rickshaw wallahs were ambushed and butchered in the adjacent cul-de-sac. Young lady, you actually watched the butchery!

WENDY

[Lost in thought] And my dear ayah was one of the butchered! How could I have forgotten? It was she who was my companion at all times; she taught me the little I know about India.

BABA

Take courage from her. She will always be at your side.

WENDY

I must be a fool to have returned. Charles, get me out of this!

CHARLES

Wendy, you've not come here to run away.

WENDY

Babaji, I really appreciate you taking the trouble to meet me. It will put my mother's mind at rest. Now, I must find somewhere to put my bag.

BABA

You will do nothing of the sort, young lady. I have booked you with Auntyji.

WENDY turns away in a huff, goes to CHARLES

CHARLES

    Who is Auntyji?

BABA

    She is the doyen of Calcutta.

CHARLES

    [In mock alarm] I'm allergic to doyens of any sort!

    Fine. That's my cue to disappear. That's why I came to Calcutta, to be a novice at the ashram where Swami Vivekananda dispersed his message to the world.

    that all religions are true. After the Holocaust, does not Europe need such a lesson?

BABA

> We all need such lessons, son. I too am a disciple of Swami Vivekananda.

CHARLES

> Maybe Babaji will point the way for me then. I must hurry to be in time for the evening service.

BABA

> *Smiles*
>
> Take a rickshaw. Tell the rickshaw wallah to get there very *slowly*! Like a pilgrim, he's on foot.
>
> Don't rush things. "The way is within you. You have to grow from the inside out. None can teach you, none can make you spiritual. There is no other teacher but your own soul."
>
> *Starts to move off.* WENDY *catches his arm*

WENDY

> I'll see you along the way ...
>
> CHARLES *picks up his bags*

Exit CHARLES *and.* WENDY

BABA *waves*

WENDY *has left her bag behind.* BABA *notices the violin and is amused*

If music be the food of love, play on, my son.

Wendy looks somewhat settled. Good to see them taking in the sounds and smells of Calcutta—tea shops, chai wallahs pouring tea from glass to empty glass. Look, Amita Bose is following them with her notebook! Good riddance!

Wendy's mother has given me her trust. No, no, I am not ignoring it. Jesus says, "No one can serve two masters." I am Baba. I can serve three, and with God included, of course it makes four! I'm using Wendy as lure to catch the big fish, hoping for Auntyji to get her into the club. Because I'm sure it's there where the problem lies. Wendy's ayah told me that whenever Wendy went to the club, she came back a different child.

Car horn sounds

Auntyji! And—oh dear—she has brought her rascal son, Rohan.

Enter ROHAN. ROHAN *freezes*

Enter WENDY

To WENDY

Your friend went off all right?

WENDY

> He kissed me goodbye. Nice little touch, eh?

BABA

> Let me help you with your bags.
>
> *As* WENDY *and* BABA *are moving* WENDY's *luggage to the side, they freeze*
>
> *Enter* AUNTYJI, *who appears gaudy in a shiny sari, heavy make-up, and much jewellery.*
>
> *Enter* ROHAN, *heavy-eyed*

AUNTYJI

> Do you like her, Rohan?

ROHAN

> [Grumpily] Kind of.

AUNTYJI

> Shall I bring her to you, Rohan? All the club ladies will be so jealous.

ROHAN

> I'll play with her my way.

AUNTYJI

> My sari is OK?

Mimes saying hello to WENDY *with exaggerated enthusiasm.* ROHAN *approves*

Rohan, go get her a rose.

Exit ROHAN

AUNTYJI

I really have to meet Wendy.

BABAJI

That is why I brought you here.

AUNTYJI

Parents?

BABAJI

[Aside] I daren't reveal John and Belinda Jones.

To AUNTYJI

Very posh diplomats, the Fotheringtons. Unfortunately, they died in an accident.

AUNTYJI

Good. That's the way we like it.

To WENDY

You must be Wendy. I am Auntyji. Welcome, child. Welcome to new India. Baba sent me note and say you are here. I rush to come examine you as soon as I get good news.

> AUNTYJI *holds* WENDY's *hand and chucks her chin. She circles the girl, patting her at in appropriate places.* WENDY *squirms*

Little darling! Baba told me you ask for help. He wants me to guard … I mean look after you while you are here.

WENDY

[Stiffly] Did he now? It's very kind of you, but I'm well able to look after myself.

AUNTYJI

No girl is safe without a man. Baba knows it.

WENDY

> *Glares at* BABA

> *To* AUNTYJI

I am quite capable of handling myself.

BABA

She only thinks of you as a beautiful English rose, my dear. Bengalis love beauty and gardens.

> *To* AUNTYJI

Look at yours.

AUNTYJI

Yes. I made mine the best. With the mocking ladies of the club watching, a village girl has to win! That's right! Gardens! Mali!

Enter CHARLES, *dressed as* MALI. CHARLES *squats on the ground*

[Ordering CHARLES in an abrupt manner] Mali, stand up! See my beautiful English rose. Water it, smell it, touch it.

Kicks CHARLES

Play ringa ringa roses with your new memsahib, like me and my little Rohan like to do.

Sings

Ringa ringa roses … and we all fall down!

Fall down, Mali!

MALI *runs away in horror*

So let us talk about new India.

WENDY

You must be happy with the new Nehru.

AUNTYJI

Who's Nehru?

BABA

Your prime minister!

AUNTYJI

Oh. Your prime minister very happy with new India!

BABA and WENDY

>No!

Auntyji

>Baba! Bring Rohan.
>
>*Exit* BABA

WENDY

>How do you know Baba?

AUNTYJI

>He's our family sadhu.
>
>*Enter* ROHAN *and* BABA
>
>Oh, there is Rohan.
>
>*To* ROHAN
>
>Look at Wendy. Like to play ringa ringa roses with her?

ROHAN

>Hello, Wendy. Welcome to India. I hope you don't mind, my mother would have us play.
>
>ROHAN *and* WENDY *play ringa ringa roses and freeze after falling*

AUNTYJI

>Now we bring this one home. You say you do it your way. It not working. This time no mistake.
>
>WENDY *and* ROHAN *unfreeze.* WENDY, *feeling distinctly uncomfortable, starts to walk off.* AUNTYJI *stops her*
>
>Don't run away. This is New Market. I buy you a beautiful sari.
>
>*Exit* WENDY *and* AUNTYJI

ROHAN

>*To* BABA
>
>Did she come with anyone else?

BABA

>[Lying] No, she came by herself.

ROHAN

>I will not tolerate second-hand goods. Every Calcutta boy will be after her. Everyone suspicious must be exterminated.

BABA

>You cannot exterminate the whole country.

ROHAN

>[Threateningly] Why not, if I wish to?! Never try to cheat me, or else your commission goes.
>
>*Enter* AUNTYJI *and* WENDY

AUNTYJI

>But you can't miss our polo match. Rohan's the captain. And after the match, the party! The party is good.
>
>*Sings a few phrases*
>
>I need matching handbag for your sari. Come, come.
>
>*Exeunt*

ROHAN

>Keep buying what you want, I'm having her only if she has enough money.

AUNTYJI

>We are now out of New Market, and it has stopped raining. Look, that is Globe Cinema, and they are showing *Bhowani Junction*. It's about an Anglo-Indian girl. These half-bake people are like mosquitos in my Calcutta.
>
>WENDY *shows interest in a poster of a voluptuous Ava Gardner, considered the most beautiful woman in the world*

ROHAN

> You've told me a hundred times about them—your husband's secretaries and all that.

AUNTYJI

> Shut up.

ROHAN

> You know it's true. Come on.

AUNTYJI

> Tits bulging, always available.

ROHAN

> (he places his hand on her shoulder)
>
> Relax, Ma—you'll get ill.

AUNTYJI

> Leave me.

WENDY

> She's beautiful.

ROHAN

> No! She is pretending to be English, which this half-breed is not.

AUNTYJI

> (She nods)

AUNTYJI

> These Anglo-Indians! *Chi chi*—oh! I have to get ready for polo lunch. Wendy, look around and then my driver will bring you home. Rohan! We take taxi back.
>
> *Exit* AUNTYJI *and* ROHAN, AUNTYJI *singing*

WENDY

> *To* BABA
>
> What the hell have you thrust upon me? That lady is incredibly annoying. You expect me to stay with them? You must have put this nonsense into action the moment you found out I was coming. I would have been better off with Charles in that funny place he has chosen. Get me out of here this minute! Or I'll walk away.

BABA

> And go where? You've barely arrived and have no idea where to go. Charles has chosen the path of knowledge. You mock his books, but they will give him direction. I visit Belur Math too from time to time. But it's not for you. Your journey is different.

WENDY

> And who's planning this absurd journey? That pantomime dame or you?

BABA

>   Those are silly people. Don't mind them; they mean no harm.

WENDY

>   What has really pointed a bullet between my eyes is your behaviour. I trusted you as a holy man.
>
>   *Picks up her bag and starts to leave*

BABA

>   So did your mother, and she has known me for much longer. Trust me, as she does. She has asked me to help you. Her request is sacred to me. Go to Flury's. You know the place! All your people went there. It's still the best Swiss confectionary south of Suez.

WENDY

>   [Defiantly] I'll go wherever I want. I wish to travel.
>
>   *Exit*

BABA

>   If that's what she wants, I'll take her travelling. For now I must follow her—don't know where she'll go. She is not safe in this city.
>
>   *Exit*

SCENE 2
Hijra's Home under the Sky

Sound of a river

Enter CHARLES, *in shorts, with a towel over his shoulder.*

HIJRA *is reclining, comfortably sprawled, drinking a glass of milk*

HIJRA

[In a good mood] *Arre gore*, white man! What are you doing here?

CHARLES

Going for a walk after prayers at the Math. What are you doing here?

HIJRA

> [Alluding to bhaang, a sweet cannabis preparation] Spending the money you gave me.
>
> *Points, laughing at* CHARLES
>
> No clothes? *Nanga bhaang* naked by the Ganga?

CHARLES

> It's so hot. I need to cool down. I need a swim.

HIJRA

> River very beautiful, but dangerous! Monsoon season! I know. I live here, under the tree—our home—with others like me. Outcasts—male and female all in one!
>
> *Takes a sip*
>
> I'll show you.
>
> *Begins to lift his sari*

CHARLES

> No! You mustn't!

HIJRA

> No work, no chance. *Kya Karein.* What to do? I was stolen, so my goolies were chopped off.
>
> Nobody will allow us in except the Math over there. We dance; they give us food. Come dance with me tomorrow—we do it for a living. You gave me money today. You are my friend.

Starts humming

Nobody wants us. I feel safe here.

Dozes off

CHARLES *settles* HIJRA *very gently.*

SCENE 3
Flury's Cake Shop

WENDY

Flury's!

Looks around

Such a grand place, posher than I remembered.

So many memories of Sarah and me eating delicious food.

(Calls out)

"Wendy! Wendy! Chocolate cake!" "No, Sarah, only one." Those days, how good they were! Father Christmas came every year to the Victoria Club giving out presents, unwrapping them before my ayah. ... I remember ladies in expensive frocks gossiping with each other, and men in moustaches winking at me.

Shudders

I never knew what to do when that happened: wink back, or run away? I just froze.

And then, when evening came, there was something that always intrigued me. Ladies sitting down after six o'clock to gin and tonic sundowners on the veranda, where we children were not allowed!

"Why? What happens there?" I asked. My ayah pulled me back. "Baby, such things are not for you."

My dear Gurkha ayah! I still long for her motherly touch, the comfort of her hand resting on mine. … Just a minute!

Pauses

Hazy memories are returning. All was not bright and beautiful at the club. These people treated me differently, even the bearers. I was sometimes in tears. My ayah would tell me that there was nothing wrong with me. She said those things happened because I was Anglo-Indian. Like a rush, a storm swept over me when that Auntyji and Rohan started going on and on about Anglo-Indians. The insult that poured from their mouths disgusted me. For the first time, I wanted to stand up and be counted.

Stands and declaims

Look, you superior bastards. I am an Anglo-Indian. With all your supposed knowledge about my people, you didn't even recognise me! I could throw this cream cake in the middle of your superior face!

Mimes a successful throw

Of course, I always knew I was Anglo-Indian, but I never realised that it mattered.

Yawns

I wish Charles was with me still. Maybe I'll go and visit his place one day. I'm sure Baba will take me. But I've got to get rid of Baba.

And that Auntyji with her matchmaking and her polo. Sarah and I went to polo matches many times.

Sarah loved those horses and the army band, decorated stands, flashy cars, champagne.

Stands up and attempts to look out over the audience

Where is she?

"Sarah, Sarah, be careful. Do not take even one step onto the field!"

I know where she's gone! To the drinks tent, where she is hiding below the table.

More champagne … dribbling bottle tops. And then us children trying to lick the bottle tops secretly amongst the rakes and tools …

Feeling dizzy … unsteady. Ground shifting beneath me.

Widening her eyes in horror, she stutters, her lips quivering

And … and … that awful, awful white man bending over me … pushing me down, down, lower and lower, onto the floor … thick lips, cigar breath. *Oh!* … Oh my God. Oh my God!

Screams

One does *not* kiss a girl, down there! One does *not* …

Drops down onto her chair, in shock

Enter Waiter

Waiter

Madam, are you all right? There is a holy man waiting outside. I think he's crying. I think I should let him in.

WENDY *raises her head a little, eyes slightly open, and looks round. Seeing nothing, she puts her head down again*

Enter BABAJI

Waiter points out WENDY, *fast asleep. Waiter pulls up a chair alongside* WENDY *and puts her head on his shoulder*

WENDY

[Speaking as a little child, not fully aware as to who is beside her] I want to go away from *him,* from the man by the billiard table sucking my little nipples. It hurts! They are monsters!

Puts her head back on the Waiter's shoulder, sobbing

Sitar music

BABA

> *Pats* WENDY *gently*

You will find peace, little bird. You will find your nest. Everywhere in the world I see the "starless night of racism".

WENDY

[Controlling herself but speaking in a confused manner as if she were a child again] Please take me away, ayah rani, and tell me again that bedtime story about a girl everybody loved. … Once upon a time …

Drifts off

BABA

Patting WENDY

Love lives in your heart, my baby. Just listen.

Puts his arm round WENDY*'s shoulder, pulling her to him.* WENDY *falls asleep*

[Whispers] Those who are near me do not know that you are nearer to me than they are. Those who speak to me do not know that my heart is full with your unspoken words. Those who love me know that their love brings me nearer to their heart.

Dearest child, I'm your love story.

SCENE 4
Song, Blowin' in the Wind

Enter Gypsy Woman. BABA *watches her*

Sounds of bombs and missiles

Gypsy Woman

> I was standing one evening
> When I heard a sound from the future, the future,
>
> The thundering heartbeat of horror
> Humankind can never change.
>
> The glacier knocks in the cupboard,
> The desert sighs in the bed,
>
> And the crack in the circle opens
> A lane to the land of the dead.
>
> (BABA comes downstage and starts singing blowin in the wind)
>
> How many roads must a boy walk down
> Before you call him a man?
>
> How many seas must a white dove sail
> Before she sleeps in the sand?
>
> Yes, 'n' how many times must the cannonballs fly
> Before they're forever banned?

The answer, my friend, is blowin' in the wind.
The answer is blowin' in the wind.

Yes, 'n' how many times must a man look up
Before he can see the sky?

Yes, 'n' how many ears must one man have
Before he can hear people cry?

The answer, my friend, is blowin' in the wind.
The answer is blowin' in the wind.

Yes, 'n' how many deaths will it take till he knows
That too many people have died?

The answer, my friend, lies in our hands.
The answer is lying in your hand.

Exit

Gypsy Woman

The answer is lying in your hands—love, immense, infinite, broad as the sky, deep as the ocean.

SCENE 5
The River

Sound of river flowing

HIJRA

    Good morning.

CHARLES

    Good morning. I didn't see you. How are you this morning?

HIJRA

    I'm coming from Belur Math after the morning prayers. I shall take bath in the holy river. You like Belur Math much?

CHARLES

    Very much.

HIJRA

    You learn much?

CHARLES

    Yes indeed.

HIJRA

    You want sweets?

    Feeds CHARLES *sweets*

CHARLES

    Stay happy, my friend.

    Exit HIJRA

    I'm no longer Charles here. … I'm a frog.

    Goes to centre upstage as if about to give a speech. Clears his throat, tidies his clothes, and gets ready

    [With aplomb, script in hand] I'm a frog.

    Clears his throat

    I'm a frog.

    Enter BABA *and* WENDY, WENDY *wearing Indian clothes*

    CHARLES *waves to* BABA *and* WENDY

Hi! Long time, no see! Wendy, good to see you here. Babaji, welcome. They told me at the monastery that both of you were travelling.

Touches BABA's *feet. Hugs* WENDY

WENDY

(Laughing)

Only three weeks

Are you a frog, or have you become a frog after staying here?

BABA

Too many dips in the Holy Ganga.

Mimes

WENDY

It makes you purer every time you submerge. That's what they say.

BABA

Don't laugh at him, Wendy. I know exactly what he's doing. He's rehearsing Swami Vivekananda's great speech that he made in Chicago to the Parliament of the World's Religions.

WENDY

Then why is it about frogs?

CHARLES

> I'll tell you. Swami Vivekananda was an astute man. He did not want his discourse to be mixed up with symbols of other world religions. So, he remained neutral and chose frogs as his teaching tool. That way everyone would listen to his story and not get offended.

WENDY

> I'll never get offended by frogs; they're cute.

CHARLES

> (Starts performing)
>
> I am a frog. I live in a well. I was born there and brought up there. One day, another frog that lived in the sea came and fell into the well.
>
> "Where are you from?"
>
> "I'm from the sea."
>
> "The sea? How big is that? Is it as big as my well?"
>
> And he took a leap from one side of the well to the other.
>
> *Takes a clumsy leap and falls down.* BABA *helps with raising him*

WENDY

> Please don't put in any actions, Charles! You're ridiculous.

CHARLES

Ignoring WENDY, *into his act*

"My friend," said the frog from the sea, "how do you compare the sea with your little well?"

Then the frog took another leap.

Takes another leap and falls, bringing his script down with him down. WENDY *helps* CHARLES *up.* CHARLES *staggers*

"Is your sea so big?"

WENDY

[Picks up the script. Reads] "What nonsense you speak to compare the sea with your well!"

CHARLES

Lifting WENDY *off her feet*

"Well then," said the frog of the well, "nothing can be bigger than my well; there can be nothing bigger than this! This fellow is a liar, so turn him out!"

BABA

It's a very potent story that underlines, very simply, the tragedy of self-imprisoned humankind.

CHARLES

Would like to be a frog, Babaji?

BABA

> *Smiles*
>
> I'd love to be the frog of the sea, but I don't wish to be thrown out! And I have to go pay my respects at the club ...
>
> *Goes to* WENDY, *who is looking at the river*
>
> Beautiful, isn't it? But be careful. The ground underfoot is slippery.
>
> You like him, don't you?

WENDY

> Sometimes I feel like giving him a clap behind his ears. Other times he makes me laugh.

BABA

> That's called love, Miss Jones.

WENDY

> Miss Jones—I like that.
>
> *Gazes at river.* CHARLES *is in meditation*

BABA

> [*Looks out over the audience and waves*] *To* AMITA
>
> What, Amita Bose arriving on a boat?! You journalists take extreme steps to find material for your story. Hurry, let the boatman get you up quickly. This time you've caught me

red-handed matchmaking. Shh. This boy Charles has really moved on. I don't want him to go back to his country.

Looks at WENDY

My journey has so far been alone—but now a song has come into my life.

Sings "Puppet on a string"

Yes, it could be first love. Her Anglo-Indian people are leaving in hordes out of India, but this one—she has come back. I hope we are left with one example from three hundred years of Anglo-Indian society. Tee-hee, I'm not joking—hoping for the future! Grandchildren!

Exit

WENDY *walks towards* CHARLES, *who has his eyes shut in meditation*

CHARLES

You're much more confident now, Wendy! I am sorry I frightened you. You seem much more settled now.

WENDY

I have been everywhere with Babaji—he took me to meet a leper. She told me never to call her a leper. "The word carries ugliness and portrays me as unlovable. It doesn't define who I am. I became whole."

These words took me back to the central question about myself: Who am I? It was for this reason I came to India, and the leper answered it for me. I may be an outcast, but I'm not leper.

CHARLES

Takes WENDY's *hands. Takes her scarf and winds it round his hand like a bandage. Puts his hand out*

Shake hands with a leper.

Sounds of the river as CHARLES *and* WENDY *touch hands*

CHARLES *and* WENDY *sit by the river.* CHARLES *sings a sweet song.* CHARLES *and* WENDY *kiss*

Will you travel with me one day?

Music

WENDY

Of course. Babaji took me to a mountain near Darjeeling, where my ayah is from. And I stood there on Tiger Hill in total darkness, and I felt my ayah standing right beside me. And suddenly,

I saw a little **white** tent—the first ray of the rising sun. I felt my soul lit up by God! And there, at that very moment, I felt like I had conquered Everest.

SCENE 6
The Club

Drawing room. Enter AUNTYJI, *holding a wedding card*

AUNTYJI

Good! It is all done. I have sent out all the wedding invitations.

Enter BABA *and* AMITA (HIDING)

Baba, you have returned—finally. Just in time for the wedding cards. We have been looking for Wendy.

BABA

Whose wedding?

AUNTYJI

Rohan and Wendy's of course! I want Rohan to look like a raja for his wedding.

BABA

> [Alarmed] I must tell Wendy about it instantly!

AUNTYJI

> There's no need. Arranged marriages are no business of youngsters. Only job get married!
>
> *Shows BABA the card*
>
> Stay here; I am getting more cards.
>
> Oh my! It's all so exciting. In the village, we collect flowers and bind them to make garlands. Girls sing. Long hair and sweet singing gives you a good husband, especially when you are beautiful like me!
>
> *Exit, humming*

BABA

> *Looks at card*
>
> What? I never thought Auntyji would act in such a tearing hurry. No! All I wanted to do was to get Wendy into the club, not to get her married to Rohan, that venom-spitting cobra. Yes, I've made a terrible mistake. I don't know what I'll do. I must tell Wendy the truth now, face the consequences. I was

so focussed on my intrigue, I totally forgot how unpredictable that woman is!

AUNTYJI

Baba, come here. I am organising Christmas party. Two hundred guests. Twenty pound cakes. And listen, no hijras. I will shoot them.

BABA

To AMITA

From a woman of garlands, she now has claws that kill.

To AUNTYJI

But Auntyji! How could you have sent this card to everybody and not even get the name of the bride right! She is not Wendy Fotherington!

AUNTYJI

[Anxiously, angrily] What do you mean? That is the name that you gave me on the piece of paper you sent me.

BABA

It was just a memo given in a hurry to a rickshaw wallah. I didn't need to give her biography. But in a wedding card, you have to get all the details right! You've not even mentioned her parents.

AUNTYJI

What's the need? Her parents are dead.

BABA

> No, they are not dead. Wendy is the adopted child of Mr and Mrs Fotherington. Her surname by birth is Miss Wendy Jones.
>
> *Enter ROHAN, who stops and listens*
>
> I have known her parents for a long time. They were missionaries who worked with lepers. I know most of her family. They were scattered around most of the railway stations in Bengal.
>
> *AUNTYJI is stunned*

ROHAN

> Then, for heaven's sake, why did you bring that half-breed to my mother, calling her a suitable girl whom you took away!

BABA

> Your mother wanted an English rose. Doesn't Wendy look like one? She's been brought up in a British diplomat's family. Very posh.

ROHAN

> Family in railway stations all over Bengal? I know exactly whom the British employed almost exclusively. She's a chi chi? An Anglo-Indian? [Very angrily] How can I allow this low-class girl to enter my club? I shall tear to pieces these awful wedding cards.

BABA

> But your mother's already sent them.

ROHAN

> [Getting manic] What! Already sent them? Without asking me! Then we will be ruined! [Melodramatically] Roll in the secretaries bedding bosses like my father and the barroom singers with bulging tits. Why not convert our Victoria Club into Howrah Station?
>
> An Anglo-Indian guard blows the whistle, his brother revs up the engine, and we climb into a second-class carriage and get served pepper soup and rice! Ugh!
>
> *Enter* MRS BANNERJI

MRS BANNERJI

> I came here to congratulate you. I have received your wedding card, and I'm sure it will be the grandest affair in Calcutta. I can't wait to see young Rohan marry Miss Fotherington-Jones.
>
> *Points at* ROHAN
>
> Looking smart. Going to a party with Miss Fotherington? Is she here?

ROHAN

> [Off his guard] She is on a round trip of India with Babaji. I can't tell you when she will return.

MRS BANNERJI

> [Instantly suspicious] But Babaji is right here.
>
> *Points to* BABA
>
> Is she travelling alone?

AUNTYJI

> Of course she is not travelling alone. We wanted to, to get rid of her … uh … uh … for the moment, I mean. While I make arrangements.

MRS BANNERJI

> [Seeking to get to the bottom of the mystery] I don't understand. Will she be back in time for the wedding?

AUNTYJI

> [Alarmed] Oh, no, that will not be possible!

MRS BANNERJI

> [Suspicious] Why not?

AUNTYJI

> Because, because, she's got chickenpox. No, no, it's measles; that takes longer. Or is it the other way?
>
> *Bawls*

MRS BANNERJI

> *To* BABA
>
> Why is she so upset about the wedding?

BABA

> Perhaps because there will be no wedding.

MRS BANNERJI

>What?

BABA

>[Jumping in with both feet, having decided to reveal all] Because Wendy's not English. Just a half-breed Anglo like you see on the streets.

MRS BANNERJI

>That will be a disgrace for our club. I must tell everyone.
>
>*Gets out her address book and starts flipping the pages*

BABA

>Yes, check all the people you can contact.

MRS BANNERJI

>*Looking crafty, approaches* AUNTYJI, *who is crying*
>
>Any way I can help?

AUNTYJI

>Can you help me? Nobody can help me!

Mrs. Bannerji

>*To* BABA
>
>I'm a senior member of the club. I will give the information to all the members.

AUNTYJI

> *To* ROHAN
>
> Why did he lead us on?!
>
> *This is the last straw for* ROHAN

ROHAN

> *Pulls* BABAJI *by the ear, dragging him off to one side*
>
> Ah! This is too much! You snivelling bastard!
>
> *Swears in Hindi*
>
> You have set out to ruin us after we have given you a home. I'll kill you.
>
> *Puts his hands round* BABA's *throat*

BABA

> *Acts undisturbed, very self-controlled, and logical. Clenches and unclenches his hands, the only sign of his stress*
>
> I would have told you the moment I discovered it, but it was *only* on our travels she leaked it out. I was horrified. You are my employer. I have to see to *your* interests *first*. You have to marry rank and riches. I was going to spirit her out as soon as I got back. You could have told everyone she had gone off to the Himalayas to become a Buddhist nun. That would have been no disgrace, just relief felt by your friends that you had been saved from a loony. You hired me for other things too.

[Whispers] If you cannot wed, there's always the bed! Your Baba will find more! There are plenty of fish in the sea.

AUNTYJI

I tried so very hard to reach this position. I can't show my face at the club anymore! I can never be Auntyji again.

Gets up, walks directionlessly

Exit

MRS BANNERJI

I'll go home and contact the others in my address book.

ROHAN

Goes to MRS BANNERJI

There has been some misunderstanding with the cards. These printers, they make mistakes, confusing one family with another. I'll go to their office. You also go home now, Mrs Bannerji.

Closes MRS BANNERJI*'s diary and tries to usher her out*

MRS BANNERJI

[Leaving] And I shall go to the club office and sort this out. Then there will be no more Auntyji, and I will take her place. I'll do it now. There are committee elections next week. Then this ghastly Auntyji will be out! She won't be able to show her face in Calcutta again. Best she goes back to her own village [laughing] and sink into some pond!

Exit, chuckling

ROHAN

> *To* BABA

> Where is this awful girl?

BABA

> In Belur Math. I left her there.

ROHAN

> Go there and bring her back. Quickly!

> *Shoos* BABA *away, but* BABA *lingers and listens*

> It's a moonlit night, and a mighty bore will be coming up the river—a huge wall of water pushed in from the sea at high tide.

> *Chuckles*

> It's my birthday. It will be very, very romantic by the river.

> We cannot retrieve the wedding cards, but ... there can always be an accident.

BABA

> I thought I had to face the consequences. Now Wendy will be killed. Amita, what shall I do?

> *Collapses*

> *Gunshot*

ROHAN

What was that? It seems to have come from upstairs.

Exit, to investigate

Enter, in a state of shock.

Mumiji, what have you done?

Pauses

Why? Stupid, stupid mother. *Why?* I had a solution.

SCENE 7
The River

Sound of river

WENDY touches CHARLES on his shoulder. CHARLES looks at WENDY

CHARLES

Wendy, you have changed your clothes.

WENDY

Charles, I have to go back to England. Sarah needs me.

CHARLES

I understand. I have led an easy life so far. It is time to pay back my debt to society and head home for I have work to do. Wendy, I have just come back from meeting Sister Teresa!

WENDY

>I only wish I had too.

CHARLES

>Yes, she inspired me. Her parting words were like a blessing: "God doesn't require us to succeed. He only requires that you try. **That I must.**"

WENDY

>*She lays her head on his shoulder*

CHARLES

>*(Mummers into her hair)*

>Wendy, I have heard some devastating news. Khrushchev ... he has a rocket that can reach the moon. I think it's called *Sputnik*.

WENDY

>What does that mean?

CHARLES

>It means conflict, Wendy.

WENDY

>*(steps back)*

>Charles! You are being melodramatic!

CHARLES

> No, Wendy, another war is coming! I can feel it in my bones. I can see it on the horizon. I fear for our time, for our children.
>
> *Enter* BABAJI, *distressed*
>
> CHARLES *takes the card from* BABAJI*'s hand*
>
> Babaji, what is this?
>
> [Reads] Wendy, you are getting married! Auntyji, she …

WENDY

> I told you that woman is insane. Babaji, did you know about this?

BABA

> Auntyji is dead! They are making it sound at the club like it was an accident in the gunroom. But she's dead, and I have blood on my hands.

CHARLES

> Don't even use the word *blood*! You are a holy man; how can anyone say you're involved?

WENDY

> Although I didn't like the woman, she was doing her best for her son.

BABA

> I *am* involved! It was my action that started the ball rolling. I am guilty in every way. I have been commanded by Rohan to take Wendy to the river for a romantic stroll—only to be murdered!

CHARLES

> The story gets better and better. You are allowing your imagination to run away with you.

BABA

> It's the truth.

CHARLES

> No worries. I'm going to do something about it! I will fix this. I will inform the press. It will be headlines tomorrow! Calcutta will be agog. Maybe new India needs a little bit of democracy!
>
> *CHARLES and WENDY, in cahoots, are excited*

BABA

> Charles! Don't do it.
>
> *Walks away from CHARLES*

CHARLES

> Why not? It's a means to an end, and Rohan certainly does not mean to kill himself. Why not kill two birds with one stone? Punish Rohan yet save him at the same time—but punished

he must be. We cannot allow evil to prosper. Wendy, get ready for the finale.

BABA *moves farther away, disappointed*

As Babaji hasn't gone back to the club, Rohan will arrive here to get you. And if the Statesman Fellow does not get here in time for the bore, then "the earth is enjoyed by heroes"— this is the unfailing truth. Be a hero, Charles! Always say, "I have no fear." I will confront him.

WENDY

You can use me as bait.

CHARLES

To expose his intention. Obviously, he will deny it absolutely, the shit. It's then that you step out, Wendy. It is then that you expose him. Let's try it out. The moon is up; it's almost time for the bore. But the journalist hasn't arrived, and Rohan will be here, looking for you. Rohan has not seen me. I will play the journalist. Look, I can see him coming.

Mimes, approaching ROHAN

[In a common accent] I'm a foreign journalist. Very interesting place, this city of yours. The boss of Victoria Club lies dead in a gunroom! Now there's talk of another murder, and the corpse is not yet cold. You look very suspicious lurking around here. Are you trying to murder Wendy? I know from my paper that she was to be your bride. Our sources know exactly what went wrong. She was an Anglo, not a person that you with your superior position could tolerate.

And then he'll say …

WENDY

> [Acting like ROHAN with his accent] I don't know any Wendy.
>
> *Goes to* CHARLES *with aplomb, acting like herself*

CHARLES

> And then you'll say …

WENDY

> "Yes you do. With Babaji, you went for an evening stroll with me by the Ganges, because it is your birthday". … Listen, it's time for that romantic stroll.
>
> *Sound of bore which keeps increasing*
>
> I can see the bore approaching.
>
> Shall we start? "Will you please walk on the side nearest to the river like a gentleman and allow me to walk a safe distance away?"
>
> *Stretches out her hand towards* CHARLES

CHARLES

> It's your decision. The photographer is ready. If you are guilty, *run!* And if you are not guilty, take her hand and walk. We're watching and waiting.
>
> *Sound of a tiger's roar*
>
> WENDY *and* CHARLES *laugh*

WENDY

> That's exactly what he'll do! Vanish!

CHARLES

> *Moves towards* BABA
>
> Either way, it will make a good story!

BABA

> *Walks up to* CHARLES *and speaks very sternly*
>
> Kill no birds; use no weapons, not even your sharp brain. Take my love and move on. Life for both of you is just beginning.
>
> *Go bravely. Do not expect success in a day or a year. Be eternally faithful to the cause of truth, humanity, and your country, and you will move the world.* I give you Vivekananda Nanda's blessing.
>
> And if you love me, *please leave now!*

Enter Amita Bose who conceals herself from them and listens intently.

> WENDY *approaches*

WENDY

> Who are you, Babaji?

BABA

> No one special. I am just a glow-worm, here to show you the way to the rainbow.

From horizon to horizon, she arches her arms, snuggling the growing world nested in her loving bosom. The soul too has a rainbow. Children, it is there for you to touch.

WENDY

Touch a rainbow? Like a child would like to do?

BABA

Only children can be innocent and wise at the same time.

On the seashore of endless worlds children meet.

I will not walk beside you anymore.

WENDY

Is this goodbye?

BABA

Looks at WENDY *and* CHARLES *for some time with the greatest of empathy*

There is no such word.

WENDY and **CHARLES** *lock onto each other and exit*

BABA

Smiles

AMITA BOSE *is already on stage left, seated, listening to the whole story*

There, Amita, I've told you the whole story. We sit by the banks of this holy river. She is meant to wash our sins away, but the question is, have I sinned?

AMITA

You are still a glow-worm. You are such a learned man. Why beg like a sadhu?

BABA

That—a gimmick to attract tourists.

AMITA

Why Gandhi?

BABA

That's the way I'd like to be.

AMITA

I've got my story.

Starts to leave. Turns back around

Perhaps Rohan will come back.

BABA

That will be another story. Perhaps you will write it.

Exit AMITA, smiling

Looks up to the sky. Rohan *will* come. Uparwala, you have given me the strength to face whatever comes. You brought Wendy as my little sister. And in Charles I found a young me.

[Childlike] I'm a child who wants to touch a rainbow, if you please.

About the Author

Pramila Le Hunte, the heady girl dashing on a bike in a sari, is an inspired English teacher from Cambridge, a tragi-comedy playwright, and a Jackie-in-the-box politician. Did marrying a Welshman make all that difference? It made her into a splendiferous, global woman, peddling along Trumpington highway.

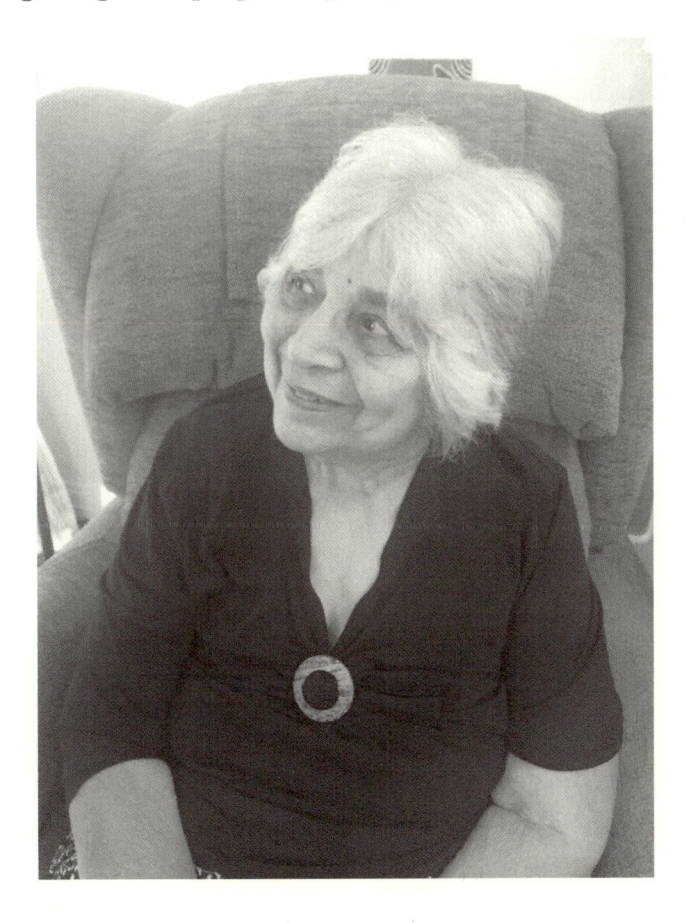